Katie Woo

Cartwheel Katie

by Fran Manushkin

illustrated by Tammie Lyon

PICTURE WINDOW BOOKS
a capstone imprint

Katie Woo is published by Picture Window Books
A Capstone Imprint
1710 Roe Crest Drive
North Mankato, Minnesota 56003
www.capstonepub.com

Text © 2015 Fran Manushkin
Illustrations © 2015 Picture Window Books

Library of Congress Cataloging-in-Publication Data
Manushkin, Fran, author.
  Cartwheel Katie / by Fran Manushkin; illustrated by Tammie Lyon.
     pages cm. — (Katie Woo)
  Summary: Katie is enrolled in a gymnastics class, but when she has trouble doing some of the moves she gets discouraged and considers dropping out.
  ISBN 978-1-4795-5894-0 (hardcover)
  ISBN 978-1-4795-5896-4 (pbk.)
  ISBN 978-1-4795-6196-4 (ebook)
1. Woo, Katie (Fictitious character)—Juvenile fiction. 2. Chinese Americans—Juvenile fiction. 3. Gymnastics—Juvenile fiction. 4. Fear of failure—Juvenile fiction. 5. Persistence—Juvenile fiction. [1. Gymnastics—Fiction. 2. Failure (Psychology)—Fiction. 3. Persistence—Fiction. 4. Chinese Americans—Fiction.] I. Lyon, Tammie, illustrator. II. Title. III. Series: Manushkin, Fran. Katie Woo.

PZ7.M3195Car 2015
813.54—dc23   2014022385

Art Director: Heather Kindseth Wutschke
Graphic Designer: Kristi Carlson

Photo Credits:
Greg Holch, pg. 26
Tammie Lyon, pg. 26

Printed in the United States of America in North Mankato, Minnesota.
122015   009389R

Table of Contents

Chapter 1

Gymnastics Class

Katie and JoJo were watching TV. Girls were doing cartwheels and jumping on trampolines.

"Those girls are cool," said JoJo.

"For sure!" said Katie.

Her mom asked, "Would you like to take a gymnastics class?"

"Yes!" yelled Katie. "Then I can be a TV star."

"That may take awhile," said her mom. "But you'll still have fun."

Katie and JoJo went to
class together.

"Welcome," said Miss
Nimble. "Let's stretch first."

"I'm great at stretching,"
bragged Katie.

"You look like my cat,"
said JoJo.

"Now let's do somersaults,"
said Miss Nimble.

"I can do those!" Katie
bragged. But she wiggled this
way and wobbled that way.

"This isn't so easy," said
Katie.

Katie wanted to do perfect
somersaults.

She practiced on the grass
with Pedro. But his puppy
did them better than she did.

It got worse the next day!

The class started

the balance

beam.

"That looks

easy," said Katie.

Oops! She kept

falling down.

"Not so easy,"

she groaned.

That night, Katie told her mom, "It's hard when it's not easy."

"That's all right," said her mom. "You are learning."

"I know," Katie sighed. "But I want to learn faster."

Chapter 2

Upside-Down Katie

At the next class, Miss

Nimble said, "We are a

team. We work together and

help each other."

"I need a lot of help,"

said Katie.

JoJo showed Katie how to do better somersaults. Katie tried again and again.

"Yay!" Katie cheered. "I'm not sideways anymore. I am upside down."

At the next class, Miss
Nimble said, "Today we will
begin cartwheels. They are
tricky but lots of fun."

Mattie did great cartwheels.

But Katie fell to the right.

Then she fell to the left.

"I don't like cartwheels," she

decided. "They are silly."

"Don't give up," said

Mattie.

"I'm not giving up," said

Katie. But she was.

After class, Katie watched

her mom playing tennis.

Sometimes she hit the

ball. Sometimes she missed.

Katie asked her, "Don't you feel sad when you miss?"

"A little," said her mom. "But I keep getting better. I am proud of me."

Chapter 3
"I Think I Can!"

At the next class, Katie

watched JoJo do cartwheels.

Sometimes she did them.

Sometimes she fell.

But she kept trying.

Katie said, "Maybe I'll try again. I'll pretend I am the Little Engine That Could."

Katie said, "I think I can! I think I can!"

But she couldn't.

"Don't give up," said JoJo.

Katie tried a second

cartwheel and a third.

She kept falling.

"Try one more," said

Mattie.

Katie tried again.

She did it!

"I did it!" Katie yelled. "I

did it. I am proud of me."

"Yay!" said Miss Nimble.

"Now we will start the trampoline," said Miss Nimble. "Who wants to try?"

"Hmm," thought Katie. "That looks tricky."

"I'll try it!" decided Katie.

She was first in line.

About the Author

Fran Manushkin is the author of many popular picture books, including *Baby, Come Out!*; *Latkes and Applesauce: A Hanukkah Story*; *The Tushy Book*; *The Belly Book*; and *Big Girl Panties*. There is a real Katie Woo — she's Fran's great-niece — but she never gets in half the trouble of the Katie Woo in the books. Fran writes on her beloved Mac computer in New York City, without the help of her two naughty cats, Chaim and Goldy.

About the Illustrator

Tammie Lyon began her love for drawing at a young age while sitting at the kitchen table with her dad. She continued her love of art and eventually attended the Columbus College of Art and Design, where she earned a bachelor's degree in fine art. After a brief career as a professional ballet dancer, she decided to devote herself full time to illustration. Today she lives with her husband, Lee, in Cincinnati, Ohio. Her dogs, Gus and Dudley, keep her company as she works in her studio.

Glossary

cartwheels (KART-weels)—circular sideways handstands

gymnastics (jim-NASS-tiks)—physical exercises, often performed on special equipment, that involve difficult and controlled body movement

somersaults (SUHM-ur-sawlts)—moves where you tuck your head into your chest and roll in a complete circle forward

stretches (STRECH-ez)—exercises where you spread out your arms, legs, or body to full length

trampolines (tram-puh-LEENS)—pieces of canvas attached to frames by elastic ropes or springs

wobbled (WOB-uhld)—moved unsteadily from side to side

Discussion Questions

1. Katie has to work extra hard at gymnastics. Have you ever had to practice extra to become good at something? Talk about it.

2. Why is it important to put in extra practice sometimes?

3. Is it ever okay to quit an activity? Why or why not?

Writing Prompts

1. Think about how Katie was having a hard time doing her gymnastics. Write a letter to her to encourage her to keep trying.

2. Write down at least five words that describe how Katie might have felt throughout the story.

3. Imagine you are a gymnast getting ready for your first competition. You are dressed and ready to go. Write a paragraph or two that describes the scene and how you feel.

Having Fun with Katie Woo!

Whenever you practice extra, you are a true champion. This gold medal is the perfect way to remind yourself that trying your best is what makes you a winner!

Be-Your-Best Medal

What you need:

- jar lid
- foam brush
- glossy Mod Podge
- gold glitter
- hot glue gun and glue
- a 2-foot-long piece of 1-inch-wide ribbon

What you do:

1. Apply a thin layer of Mod Podge over the front and sides of the jar lid.

2. Sprinkle glitter all over the Mod Podge. Let dry.

3. Shake off any extra glitter. If you would like your medal to be more glittery, repeat steps 1 and 2.

4. Apply a final layer of Mod Podge over the medal to seal in the glitter. Let dry completely.

5. Ask a grown-up to hot glue the ends of the ribbon to the back of the medal, making a loop that can go around your neck.

Congratulations, champion! Keep up the hard work!

THE FUN DOESN'T STOP HERE!

Discover more at www.capstonekids.com

- 💜 Videos & Contests
- ❀ Games & Puzzles
- 💜 Friends & Favorites
- ❀ Authors & Illustrators

Find cool websites and more books like this one at www.facthound.com. Just type in the Book ID: **9781479558940** and you're ready to go!